W9-AOE-860

01/2020

DISCARD

# A Place for Everything

## SEAN COVEY

Illustrated by **Stacy Curtis**

Ready-to-Read

Simon Spotlight
New York  London  Toronto  Sydney  New Delhi

To my sons Michael Sean,
Nathan, Weston, and Wyatt:
May you never lose
your love for good shoes!
—Sean Covey

 To my mom,
for teaching me to pick up my stuff.
—Stacy Curtis

SIMON SPOTLIGHT
An imprint of Simon & Schuster Children's Publishing Division
1230 Avenue of the Americas, New York, New York 10020
This Simon Spotlight edition December 2019
Copyright © 2010 by Franklin Covey Co.
All rights reserved, including the right of reproduction in whole or in part in any form.
SIMON SPOTLIGHT, READY-TO-READ, and colophon are registered trademarks of Simon & Schuster, Inc.
For information about special discounts for bulk purchases, please contact Simon & Schuster Special
Sales at 1-866-506-1949 or business@simonandschuster.com.
Manufactured in the United States of America 1119 LAK
2 4 6 8 10 9 7 5 3 1
CIP data for this book is available from the Library of Congress.
ISBN 978-1-5344-4451-5 (hc)
ISBN 978-1-5344-4450-8 (pbk)
ISBN 978-1-5344-4452-2 (eBook)

One day Jumper Rabbit
bounced by Uncle Bud's Park.
Pokey Porcupine, Stink Skunk,
and Tagalong Allie
were playing a pick-up game
of basketball with some badgers.

They asked Jumper to play.
"You bet," said Jumper.

"You can't play without sneakers,"
said Allie.
Jumper was wearing flip-flops.
"I'll race home and get
my favorite basketball sneakers
right now," said Jumper.

But Jumper's rabbit hole was a mess.
He couldn't find his sneakers
anywhere.
He looked in his closet.

He looked under his bed.

He looked in all his sports gear.

Jumper started tossing things
out of his rabbit hole.
He tossed out balls, toys,
gloves, and more!

Just then
Goob Bear walked by,
and Jumper's soccer ball hit him.

Goob yelled, "Ouch!
What are you doing, Jumper?"

Jumper said, "I can't find
my favorite basketball sneakers,
and I need them right now!"

Goob suggested they go back
to the places Jumper had been.
They raced across Cherry Creek
to Lily's burrow.
The sneakers were not there.

They looked for them
at Sammy and Sophie's tree house.
The sneakers were not there.

They dug up Allie's sandbox.
The sneakers were not there.

They stopped by Pokey's place.
The sneakers were not there.

They even looked
in Goob's cave.
They did not find
the sneakers.

"I'll *never* be able to play basketball again for the rest of my LIFE!" wailed Jumper.

Goob suggested they look
in Jumper's rabbit hole again.
Goob cheered up his friend
as they walked back
to Jumper's home.

At Jumper's, Goob said,
"No wonder you can't
find your sneakers.
Your room looks like a tornado hit it.

My dad taught me:
'a place for everything and
everything in its place.'"
"What does that mean?"
asked Jumper.

"It means you have to organize
your things so you can find them.
Otherwise you waste
a lot of time looking for stuff,"
said Goob.
"Oh," said Jumper. "Can you help
me do that?"

It took a long time
to clean up the hole.
Finally they found
the basketball sneakers.
They were under a big heap
of smelly clothes.
Jumper and Goob also found other
missing things, like the silver dollar
that Jumper's grandpa gave him.

They raced back to Uncle Bud's
Park, but the game was all over.
"Bummer," said Jumper.

"Don't worry, Jumper—
you'll be ready next time,"
said Goob.
Goob invited Jumper
to look for ladybugs.
He just needed to find
his magnifying glass!
Luckily, Jumper knew where it was!

## Up for Discussion

1. Why couldn't Jumper play basketball with his friends?
2. What happened when Jumper went back to his home to find his favorite basketball sneakers?
3. What important lesson did Goob teach Jumper about finding stuff?
4. How did Jumper feel when he cleaned his room and found his basketball sneakers?
5. Why is it important to be organized and have a "place for everything and everything in its place"?

## Baby Steps

1. Do you have something important that you always lose? Find a place right now where you will always keep it.

2. Clean your room really well, and then invite a parent to come see. Watch how happy they get!

3. Do you have a place for all your homework? If not, ask a parent to help you make a special place to keep it.

4. Shoes are important, so find a good place to keep your shoes every night.

5. Talk to your parents about how they take care of their things.

# PARENTS' CORNER

## HABIT ③ —Put First Things First: *Work First, Then Play*

My son Weston is the king of losing shoes. And they always seem to disappear when we're late for an important date. Sometimes we find them by the trampoline, soaking wet from the sprinklers, or in the backseat of the car, stuffed with French fries from the night before. Too often we never see them again. For sure, a little organization would save a whole lot of time, money, and frustration.

Have you ever packed a suitcase and noticed how much more you can fit when you neatly fold and organize your clothes instead of just throwing them in? It's really quite surprising. The same goes for our lives. The better organized we are, the more we are able to pack in—more time for family and friends, more time for work, more time for play, more time for our "first" things.

This is what Habit 3: Put First Things First is all about. It's about working before we play and keeping our lives organized. Learning basic organization skills is a good thing at any age, but especially while young. That's why we ought to teach our kids that just as there is a time for everything—a time for work, a time for play, and a time for sleep—there should also be a place for everything—a place for our shoes, a place for our homework, and a place for our toys.

In this story, be sure to point out how badly Jumper felt when he missed playing basketball with the gang because his room was so messy he couldn't find his shoes. Contrast that with how good he felt when his room was clean and organized.